Something Really Scary?

You'd better be if you're walking along Fear Street. Where every shadow hides a new nightmare. A different terror. People have seen ghosts in Fear Mansion. Ghouls in the Fear Street Cemetery. And monsters rising from the depths of Fear Lake.

Monsters . . . Wes Parker can tell you what it's like to see one of those.

All Wes wanted to do was find the 3-D image in his Mystery Poster. But when he discovers what's hidden there, he realizes something truly terrible. The creature in the poster is staring right back at Wes . . . and drooling.

Are you ready to see what Wes sees?

Also from R. L. Stine

The Beast
The Beast 2

R. L. Stine's Ghosts of Fear Street

#1 Hide and Shriek
#2 Who's Been Sleeping in My Grave?
#3 Attack of the Aqua Apes
#4 Nightmare in 3-D

Available from MINSTREL Books

NIGHTMARE IN 3-D

A Parachute Press Book

A
MINSTREL®
BOOK

Published by POCKET BOOKS
New York   London   Toronto   Sydney   Tokyo   Singapore

A MINSTREL PAPERBACK *Original*

 A Minstrel Paperback published by
POCKET BOOKS, a division of Simon & Schuster Inc.
1230 Avenue of the Americas, New York, NY 10020

Copyright © 1996 by Parachute Press, Inc.

NIGHTMARE IN 3-D WRITTEN BY GLORIA HATRICK

ISBN: 0-671-52944-7

First Minstrel Books printing January 1996

10 9 8 7 6 5 4 3 2

FEAR STREET is a registered trademarks of Parachute Press, Inc.

A MINSTREL BOOK and colophon are registered trademarks of Simon & Schuster Inc.

Cover art by Broeck Steadman

Printed in the U.S.A.

R·L·STINE'S
GHOSTS of FEAR STREET ®

NIGHTMARE IN 3-D

1

"**Y**ou have to cross your eyes, Wes."

"No, you don't, Wes. You just have to cross one eye."

"That's wrong, you jerk. Just stare at the two dots until they look like three dots, Wes. Then look at the whole picture and you'll see it."

The "it" everybody was talking about was a stereogram—one of those pictures with a hidden 3-D image. Mr. Gosling showed us one in our sixth-grade science class today. We're studying optics and learning about how we see things.

It was lunchtime now, and my best friend,

Lauren, and two other kids in my class were trying to give me tips on how to see stereograms. But I knew they were wasting their time.

I mushed my gravy into my mashed potatoes and slid the carrots to one side of my plate. The carrots in the school cafeteria are always soggy.

"It's no use," I said, pushing my glasses up. "I just can't see 3-D."

"You can, Wes," Lauren insisted. "It just takes some practice. You'll get it."

That's what I like about Lauren. She thinks positive. Another thing I like about her is her bright blue eyes. They look so cool under her black bangs.

"What will Wes get?" Cornelia Phillips demanded, shoving in next to me at the table.

Cornelia is one of the horrible twins who live next door to my family. Her horrible sister, Gabriella, strutted up right behind her.

Gabriella slid her tray across the table, then sat down, too. As if we'd invited them or something.

"What will you get, Wes?" Gabriella repeated. They're both so nosy.

Then, while they waited for my answer, they both twirled their long blond ponytails. They wear

2

them coming out of the sides of their heads, only on different sides so you can tell them apart. Otherwise they're alike in every gross detail. They even snort alike when they laugh.

And I hear them snorting a lot because, as I said, the twins live next door to me—on Fear Street. Everyone has stories about the scary things that happen on Fear Street. But if you ask me, the twins are the scariest things on the block!

They're worse than the ghost that everyone says plays hide-and-seek with you in the woods—and tries to steal your body. Or that ghostly substitute teacher my friend Zack had.

I call the twins Corny and Gabby. Perfect names. Corny's always playing dumb practical jokes, mostly on me. She'll do anything to make me look like a total idiot.

And Gabby's always talking. She's the biggest gossip at Shadyside Middle School. And guess who most of her stories are about? That's right—me. Wes Parker.

"What will Wes get?" the twins demanded together, their voices growing higher and higher.

I tried to ignore them. That's what Lauren always tells me to do. I stared down at my plate and mashed my potatoes around some more.

3

When no one answered, Corny finally changed the subject.

"Did you ever see anything grosser than that cow eye Mr. Gosling dissected?" she asked. Then she wrinkled her nose and gazed at everyone. Waiting for an answer.

"We're eating lunch, Cornelia," Lauren reminded her.

"Yeah, I thought it was going to squirt right off the table when he cut it open," Gabby added, ignoring Lauren.

Lauren and I groaned and dropped our forks. The twins snorted together.

"Hi, Chad." Corny waved at Chad Miller at the next table. He's one of the cool kids. Chad didn't even glance at her.

"Hey, he smiled at you!" Gabby said. She twirled her hair with one hand and stuffed her face full of potatoes with the other.

Lauren rolled her eyes.

"Wow. This table is bor-ring!" Corny groaned.

"Yeah," Gabby agreed. She reached into her backpack and pulled out a poster. She spread it out on the table, practically pushing my tray off.

Oh, no, I thought. Another stereogram. The other kids leaned over to study it.

"Can you see it, Wes?" Corny asked in a fake sweet voice.

She knew I couldn't. I never can see them. But I stared at the poster and tried hard to see the hidden image.

No use.

"Uh-uh," I admitted. I felt really stupid. The twins can always do that to me. "I can't see it. I just can't see it."

Corny leaned across my tray. She was right in my face. "Well, then, you'd better eat your carrots."

Gabby rolled the poster up and both twins left, whispering to each other and snorting some more.

"They think they're a riot," I grumbled. "Eat my carrots. Very funny."

I gazed down at my carrots.

Gasped in disbelief.

And then let out a scream that shook the room.

2

My carrots stared back at me!

An enormous eyeball poked up from the middle of them.

I shoved my chair away from the table. It caught on a loose floor tile and flipped over backward—with me in it.

Then someone started to clap—slowly. I gazed up. It was Corny. She wore a big grin on her face.

Then Gabby joined in. With the same slow, loud clap.

Lauren helped me up. "You okay?" she asked.

I nodded and straightened my chair.

The whole cafeteria was clapping and laughing now. Even the cool kids.

I tried to smile as I sat back down.

I picked up my fork and forced myself to prod the cow eye. It rolled into the mashed potatoes.

"It's fake," I said to Lauren through clenched teeth. "It's only plastic." Then I began to stand.

"Where are you going?" she asked.

"I am going to get up—and kill the twins," I answered.

"Forget it," Lauren replied, tugging me back down. "It was just another one of the twins' stupid jokes. You have to ignore them."

I glanced around, searching the cafeteria for them, but they had vanished. "I'm not going to ignore them. Not this time," I said through clenched teeth. "This time I'm going to get even."

I still felt upset when school let out. Lauren and I decided to hang around in the Old Village before heading home.

"I don't care what you say, Lauren. This time I'm going to get back at the twins."

"What are you going to do?" she asked. "You're too cool to play any of their stupid jokes."

7

"I don't know . . ." I stopped short in the middle of the sidewalk. I felt as if someone had jerked me back by the hair. "Look!" I said, pointing into Sal's Five-and-Ten.

The twins' stereogram hung in the window. The one they showed us at lunch.

A sign over it read: MYSTERY STEREOGRAM— FIND THE HIDDEN IMAGE AND WIN A PRIZE!

"That's it!" I cried.

"What are you talking about?" Lauren asked.

"That poster is the same one the twins had at lunch," I explained. "So they must be trying to win the prize. If I can figure out the poster before they do, it will be the perfect revenge."

"All right! Let's go in!" Lauren cheered, leading the way into Sal's.

The ancient wooden floor creaked under our feet as we stepped inside. "It smells funny in here," I whispered. "Old and musty. And a little like rotting eggs."

"Whew," Lauren breathed. "It's really hot, too." She unzipped her jacket.

We wandered up and down rows of metal tables. Each was divided into sections by pieces of cardboard. None of the stuff seemed organized. Plastic

8

dolls sat next to piles of pot holders. Tubes of lipstick leaned against a stack of pocketknives.

And everything loose. Nothing came in boxes or wrapped in plastic.

"This store is really old and really weird," Lauren commented. She opened a lipstick to check the color. It was half used. Yuck.

We moved on.

Some old music played in the background. I recognized it. It sounded like the kind my grandfather plays when we visit him. Big band music, he calls it. It floated from a huge old radio.

I'd almost forgotten all about the Mystery Stereogram when a guy popped up from behind the back counter.

Lauren and I leaped back in surprise. He seemed to appear out of nowhere.

That must be Sal, I realized.

He dressed all in black and his hair was greased back. And he had an incredible mustache. It curled up and around to his cheeks. Really weird. But it wasn't the weirdest thing about him.

The weirdest thing was his eyes. They were enormous and watery, like the cow eye in class. And they bulged out from his eye sockets.

I took a step back and nearly knocked over a basket full of Mystery Stereograms. I lifted one out and unrolled it. "I . . . I want one of these," I said.

Sal blinked. "Oh. That," he snarled.

"Uh, I was wondering—how come there's a prize?"

"Is it a special kind of stereogram or something?" Lauren added.

Sal shook his head impatiently. "That has nothing to do with me." Then he turned his back to us.

I cleared my throat. "But it's in your window."

"Yes." He sighed, then spun around to face us again. "It *is* in my window. But I didn't put it there. The poster company did. They are offering the prize. I allowed them to hang it up. I thought it might bring in customers. No one wants to shop in five-and-tens anymore. Everyone is at the mall."

When he said "mall," he curled his lip and rolled his huge eyes. "I can't compete."

Lauren spread the poster out on the dusty glass counter.

I stared hard at its billions of tiny fluorescent dots. They were yellow, green, orange, and pink. But I couldn't see a picture inside it.

10

"I see only dots, Lauren," I admitted.

Lauren moved closer to the poster, then backed away. Then she smiled. "No big deal, Wes. Neither can I."

Sal reached out and grabbed the poster. "Good. Then that's settled." He started to shove it under the counter.

"But I want it," I protested. I had to get my revenge on the two monsters of Fear Street. "I have to figure out how to see it."

Sal frowned. "You can see it. You need only three things to see a stereogram."

I waited, holding my breath. Finally, someone was going to tell me the secret.

"You need a right eye. A left eye. And a brain." He smiled for the first time. He had big teeth, like a horse.

Some secret, I thought. Did he think I'd been trying to see stereograms without my brain? I handed my money over to Sal.

"You better be careful," he warned as he rang up the sale on his noisy old-fashioned cash register.

"Be careful of what?" Lauren asked.

Sal moved around the counter to stand close to me. He placed his face right up to mine and opened his eyelids wide. His big eyes bulged out more than ever now. I could see all these tiny red veins running through his eyeballs.

I tried to back away, but the basket of rolled-up posters stood directly behind me.

Sal stared at me so hard I felt as though he had X-ray vision. *"You* have the power to see more than most of us," he said in a creepy whisper.

I slid sideways to move away from him. This guy was beyond weird. "No, uh, I can't really see well at all. That's why I wear glasses."

"I am not talking about twenty-twenty eyesight. I am talking about true vision. *The power to see."*

He hissed the word *see* and his eyes bulged out even farther.

"Uh, it's getting kind of late," Lauren said. "We'd better get going, Wes." She smiled nervously.

I grabbed the poster from Sal. Then Lauren and I practically jogged down the aisle to the door. I gripped the door handle and pulled the door open—but a huge hand flew over my shoulder and slammed it shut.

I spun around.

Sal stared hard at me.

"Remember," he said again in that scary whisper. "*You* have the power to see. And some things are better left in two dimensions."

Lauren and I opened the door and hurried onto the sidewalk.

What did he mean by that? I wondered.

Why was he trying to scare me?

3

I was still trying to figure out what Sal meant when I reached home. *"You* have the power to see." Why did he keep saying that to me—and not to Lauren?

And why did he warn me to be careful?

I threw my jacket over one of the kitchen chairs and spread the Mystery Stereogram out on the table. I pinned it down with the salt and pepper shakers.

I stared and stared. "You have the power to see," Sal's words repeated in my head.

Ha! What did he know?

I couldn't see a thing.

I rubbed my eyes, wiped my glasses on my flannel shirt, and tried again.

I gazed at the poster close up.

I stepped back and stared at it from far away.

Close up again.

Then far away.

"What on earth are you doing?" Mom asked as she walked through the kitchen door, struggling with two huge bags of groceries. "Didn't you hear me honking the horn?"

"No. Sorry, Mom." Boy, I must have really been concentrating!

I went out to the car for the last two bags of groceries. As I entered the kitchen, Clawd, our cat, streaked between my legs and bolted through the kitchen and into the living room. He nearly sent me flying.

Outside I could hear a dog's annoying yipping. It was Fluffums, the twins' nasty little dog.

Fluffums attacks Clawd every chance he gets. He hates Clawd. It figures.

"Look what I bought," I said as Mom started unpacking the groceries. "It's a poster. I got it at the weird five-and-ten store in the Old Village."

15

Mom stopped and sniffed. "What's that horrible smell?"

I sniffed. "I think it's my poster. It smells like the store."

"Sal's Five-and-Ten?" she asked. "I haven't been in that strange little store in years."

"It's strange all right," I said. "Especially Sal." I sat down at the table. "Take a look at the poster."

Mom glanced at it.

"Cool, huh?" I asked.

"It really stinks," Mom said, covering her nose.

"Yeah, I know. But look at it, Mom. It's called a stereogram. And if you stare at it the right way, you can see a three-dimensional image hidden in it."

Mom folded a bag and leaned over the poster. "All I can see are a bunch of colored dots."

As Mom peered closer at it, my little sister, Vicky, ran into the kitchen. "Hey, Mom! Did you buy Froot Loops? Can I have a bowl now? Hey—is that 3-D?"

Vicky always does that. Asks a whole load of questions, one on top of the other. She doesn't even give you time to answer.

"Yes, no, and yes," Mom said. She's used to Vicky and her questions.

But Vicky wasn't even listening. She was staring at my poster. "Cool," she said, pushing her glasses up her nose. "There's one of these on the back of my cereal box. I'll show you." She reached up to the counter cabinet and pulled the box down.

We all studied it. It had lots of red and blue squiggles.

"It says there's a mouse hidden in the picture," Vicky said, "and I can see it. It's a big mouse."

I stared at the box. All I could see were the squiggles. "Hey, how do you do that?" I asked. I couldn't believe my little sister could see it and I couldn't.

Vicky shrugged. "I kind of cross one eye, like this." She peered up, and sure enough, behind her glasses I could see one eye gazing straight at me. The other was staring at her nose.

"Stop that, Vicky!" Mom exclaimed. "Your eyes will stay like that."

Vicky uncrossed her eye. "It says on the cereal box there are other ways to do it, too."

I read the directions off the back of the box.

17

"Press your nose against the picture. Then, very slowly, pull it away. Don't blink. As you look deeply into the picture, a 3-D image will appear!"

I tried it. No luck. Just a bunch of fat squiggles.

Mom tried it. "I feel silly." She laughed. She slowly pulled the cereal box away from her face. "No. Wait. I've got it! There is a mouse! He's eating something!"

I couldn't believe it. They had to be teasing me.

"Here. Try it again, Wes," Mom said to me. "It really works."

I held the box close, pressing it against my nose. The tiny red and blue designs were a blur. I pulled the box away slowly, my eyes wide open. Not blinking.

But I could feel my eyes struggling to refocus. And that's exactly what they did.

I was staring at squiggles.

No mouse.

No 3-D image.

I felt totally frustrated. "Okay," I said, holding the box up in front of them. "If both of you can see it so well, what's the mouse eating?"

Mom and Vicky peered at the picture together.

"Come on," I said. "What's it eating?"

"Swiss cheese," they sang out together.

18

I slammed the box on the table. "I'll do it," I silently promised myself. "Even if it kills me."

Clawd wandered back into the kitchen and jumped onto my lap. He tilted his head as he stared at the cereal box. Then he took a swipe at it, knocking the box over.

"I don't believe it!" I shouted. "Even the cat can see 3-D! Wait a second. If you're all so smart, tell me what's in this picture," I commanded.

I stood up and stabbed my finger at the Mystery Stereogram. Clawd jumped down and darted to a corner in the kitchen.

Mom and Vicky studied the poster. I could see Vicky crossing one eye again.

Mom shook her head. "No. I can't do that one."

Vicky's face was practically touching it. "Yuck!" she cried, backing away. "This thing smells like something rotten."

"Hah! You can't see it, either!"

"Let Clawd try," Vicky suggested. She carried it over to Clawd's corner, where he was licking a paw.

She held the poster up in front of him. He stopped licking his paw, but for a second he didn't put it down. He just kind of froze in place. And stared.

Then all his fur stood out. He looked as if he'd been in the clothes dryer or something. He arched his back and opened his mouth so wide that I could see every single one of his teeth. Even the ones all the way in the back.

Then he hissed and tore through the catflap faster than I'd ever seen him move.

Vicky shrugged. "Guess he didn't like it."

I rolled up the poster and said I was going upstairs to my room to do my homework. But instead of studying, I took my Shaquille O'Neal poster down from the wall by my bed and hung up the Mystery Stereogram in its place.

Now I could stare at it last thing at night, first thing in the morning.

I was determined to see 3-D. I was determined to win the contest.

I was going to beat those horrible twins.

"I'll start practicing this minute," I said aloud. "Homework will have to wait."

I sat cross-legged on my bed. First I'll try Vicky's way, I thought. The one-eye-crossed method.

But I quickly found out that I'm not very good at crossing one eye. I can cross two okay. But I

20

could tell that crossing one at a time was going to take a lot of practice. And I didn't have that much time—if I was going to beat the twins.

Then I did what the cereal box said. I moved up real close to the poster. The tiny bright dots grew into a blur. Then I slowly inched backward on my bed.

I kept my eyes wide open.

I didn't blink.

My eyes started to burn. They were trying hard to focus.

I backed up a little more.

A little more.

Then—I fell out of bed.

"Wesley? What are you doing up there?" Dad was home from work.

"Just practicing my kung fu," I joked.

"Well, cut it out." Not a joke.

Clawd popped his head in the doorway.

"Come here, Clawd." I patted the bed.

The cat took a small step into the room. Then he noticed the poster. His ears flattened. His eyes narrowed. Then he turned and ran.

I flopped down on my bed and slipped off my glasses. I rubbed my eyes. They felt tired. I gazed

21

blankly at my wallpaper. The same wallpaper I've had since I was three years old. Rows and rows of toy soldiers.

Then I saw it! I couldn't believe it!

I rubbed my eyes and stared again.

Yes! One of the soldiers was moving. He was marching.

Marching off the wallpaper.

Marching toward me.

4

I bolted straight up in bed and jerked my head from the wallpaper.

I felt so dizzy. Did I really see what I thought I saw? Only one way to find out.

I slowly turned to face the wall and . . .

Nothing.

The toy soldier stood flat and still.

No marching.

No 3-D.

Same as always.

But I had seen a soldier move. I knew it.

I rubbed my eyes hard and concentrated—this time on the Mystery Stereogram. I felt my eyes relax.

Slowly all the tiny dots began to swirl. Orange, green, yellow, and pink dots flowed around the poster. Like lava spewing from a volcano.

I started to feel a little sick. The way I feel on a Ferris wheel. But I kept staring, not daring to blink.

I felt myself falling forward. As if something were trying to pull me into the poster. I grabbed a fistful of covers with each hand to anchor myself. But I didn't blink.

The dots spun around even faster. They seemed to surround me, trying to suck me in with the power of a huge vacuum cleaner.

Still—I didn't blink. And now the dots were forming a shape. A tree?

Yes! A tree!

And then I saw something in the tree. A bird? No, not a bird.

Something with a really long, skinny body. And two huge feelers.

And a big triangular head. And eyes! Two huge black eyes.

And finally I could see two long front legs

24

forming out of the dots. Two long legs with pincers on the ends!

A praying mantis!

That was it! I could see it! I could see in 3-D!

A praying mantis! Now I could claim the prize. I beat the twins!

I tried to blink, but my eyelids felt glued open. I couldn't break away.

I noticed even more details.

The mantis's jaws were large and powerful.

The eyes were wet and shiny.

It looked alive!

Something brushed against my neck. Then I felt tiny legs crawling over my cheek.

I dropped the covers and brushed the side of my face. My fingers touched something soft and fluttery. Ewww!

I swatted at it. I jerked my head back as it darted past my eyes.

A moth?

A sigh of relief escaped my lips. Get a grip, Wes, I told myself. This 3-D thing is making you jittery.

I watched the moth flutter around the room. And circle back. And hover in front of the poster.

Then something else caught my eye.

Nah. It couldn't be. No way.

I thought I saw the mantis twitch. I really *was* losing it.

I reached out and snatched the moth in midair. I held it in my fist. I could feel its wings beating against the palm of my hand.

Slowly I moved my fist to the left side of the poster.

Slowly I uncurled my fingers.

I could feel the moth crawl up my little finger. But I never tore my eyes from the mantis.

I watched it carefully.

I watched as it twisted its head to the left. I watched as it peered at the moth.

It peered at the moth!

The mantis really was alive!

Suddenly I heard Sal's words as clearly as if he stood in the room with me. "Some things are better left in two dimensions."

The moth flew from my hand and landed on the poster. Then it started crawling up the tree. Up to where the mantis lurked. Waiting.

I held my breath. My eyes began to water but I didn't dare blink. Not now.

The mantis's head moved slightly. Its feelers twitched. It held its front legs together. Just as if it were praying.

The moth climbed up the tree. Moved nearer and nearer to the mantis. Then one of the mantis's long front legs lashed out from the picture!

In one swift motion its huge pincers closed down on the moth and jerked it into the poster.

And I watched in horror as the mantis shoved the moth—wings and all—straight into its waiting mouth.

The mantis swallowed with a wet gulp.

Then its big eyes rolled hungrily toward me.

5

"**D**inner!" Mom shouted from downstairs.

I blinked.

"Wes, are you coming?" Dad hollered.

"Uh, yeah," I croaked.

My pulse raced. Something tickled my forehead. I jerked my hand up to swipe at it. Only tiny beads of perspiration dripping down my face.

I slid away from the poster and tried to stand up. My knees shook so badly I had to sit back down on the bed.

But I didn't look at the poster again. I wasn't ready.

I fumbled for my glasses and put them on with trembling hands. Calm down, I told myself. Just calm down.

When my breathing began to slow and my hands stopped shaking, I knew I had to take another peek at the poster.

Okay, here I go, I told myself firmly, trying to build up my confidence.

I slowly turned to face the poster, and my gaze was met with . . .

Colored dots.

Only colored dots.

No mantis.

And no moth.

I tried to think of a logical explanation. That's what Mr. Gosling, my science teacher, always tells us to do. But I couldn't come up with one. I decided I had to tell Mom and Dad. They were logical. Usually.

I joined my family at the dinner table. Mom had made spaghetti and garlic toast. My favorite. Too bad I wasn't hungry.

"Pass the Parmesan cheese, please," Dad said. He smiled. "Hey, I'm a poet and I don't even know it!"

"But your feet show it. They're Longfellows,"

Vicky finished for him. It was a silly game they always played.

"Uh, something strange just happened in my bedroom," I began.

"Mom, what's for dessert?" Vicky asked. "Can I have some more milk?"

"Frozen yogurt. Yes," Mom said, reaching for the milk.

"Is there any more spaghetti?" Dad asked.

They weren't paying attention to me. I had to make them listen.

"Here you go," Mom said, passing the bowl.

"I think my 3-D poster is coming alive!" I blurted out. That ought to get them.

Dad raised his eyebrows. "What do you mean, Wes?" he asked as he twirled his fork on his spoon, winding the spaghetti.

I cleared my throat. "I found a praying mantis in my poster, and it ate a moth that was flying around in my room."

"Yuck!" Vicky uttered, spitting out a mouthful of spaghetti. "That's disgusting!"

"So is that," Dad warned Vicky. He pushed his glasses up on his nose. "Wes, you probably just stared at it too hard. Your eyes can do funny things when they're tired."

"No, you don't understand," I protested. "I saw—"

Yeoow! Clawd raced through the catflap at full speed with a high-pitched screech.

Right behind him came Fluffums.

Our eyes followed the two crazed animals, but no one at the table moved. I don't think any of us could believe it. Fluffums. In our house.

Then someone pounded on the kitchen door. "Give us our dog back!" I heard one of the twins yell.

Hah! As if we'd invited the furry little rat in! For a second I didn't know whether to chase after the animals or go to the door and tell them off.

"I'll get the door," my father said.

"Wes, find Clawd," Mom ordered.

I searched the downstairs. Clawd wasn't there. So I dashed upstairs. Now I could hear Clawd yowling and Fluffums yipping. The sounds were coming from my bedroom.

When I hit the top step I froze. An agonizing yelp of pain echoed in my ears.

I tore down the hall, straight for my room. The first thing I spotted was Clawd, perched on my tall dresser. His back was arched and his fur stood straight out.

31

I gazed around the room for Fluffums. I couldn't find him.

Then I heard whimpering from the corner. The dog cowered there, his ears and tail down, his little body trembling.

Before I could make a move, the twins barreled in.

"Where's Fluffums?" Corny demanded. She shoved me out of the way. In my own room!

"Look! There! In the corner!" Gabby shouted. "I'll get him." She pushed past me, too, and reached down for the dog.

He growled. "I hope he bites her," I muttered under my breath.

"What's the matter, little Fluffums?" Gabby cooed in baby talk.

Fluffums whined and backed farther into the corner.

"Did that nasty old cat tease you again?" Corny added. She glared at Clawd—then at me.

I scooped Clawd up off the dresser. He clung to my shoulder. "Ouch!" I cried out as his claws sunk right through my shirt. He was in a real panic.

"Nasty cat." Gabby sneered, petting her dog. "He even claws his owner."

"Only when he's scared to death," I shot back.

"Come on, Baby Fluffy," Corny crooned. She swept the furball into her arms. She held him cradled in front of her like a baby.

"Oh, no!" Gabby shouted, pointing to the dog. "Look at his side! There's a patch of fur missing!"

"It was torn out!" Corny exclaimed. "By that horrible cat."

I stared at the dog's side. There *was* some fur missing. "Are you sure it wasn't missing before?" I asked. "Maybe he's going bald or something."

The twins went ballistic.

"He's not going bald, you jerk. Your stupid cat attacked him!" Corny shouted.

"We're going to tell our parents," Gabby threatened. "They've got a lawyer and he'll sue you. You and your cat and your whole family."

They stomped out of my room.

I stroked Clawd behind the ears. "You didn't do that—did you, Clawd?" I whispered. "You wouldn't hurt a fly."

Clawd started to squirm out of my arms. I let him go. He charged out of the room.

My eyes moved across the room to the poster. What was that spot on the front?

I walked over and touched it.

Then a cold chill ran down my body.

6

The spot—it was white and soft.

Furry.

A clump of Fluffum's fur!

But that was impossible!

How did it get there?

Did the praying mantis . . .

No! Impossible!

I sprinted out of my room to tell Mom and Dad.

But on the way downstairs I overheard Mom say something so awful I had to stop and listen.

"I can't imagine how Clawd would cope." Mom sounded sad. "He's not a house cat. He loves to curl up in the backyard. Don't you think it would be cruel to lock him inside?"

Dad didn't answer right away.

What is he waiting for? He knows Clawd would hate being cooped up in the house.

"We have to think about it," he said finally. "This dog and cat situation has been the cause of a lot of problems."

I felt my face get hot. I'll straighten this out, I decided. All I have to do is tell them that Clawd didn't touch the twins' dumb little dog. All I have to do is tell them that it was the mantis.

Yeah, right. A 3-D mantis. Like they'll really believe me. Anyway, they'd probably think I was making the whole thing up to get Clawd out of trouble.

I turned around and crept back up the stairs to my room. My eyes darted to the mystery poster hanging over my bed. No way did I want to go to sleep anywhere near that, I thought.

My fingers shook as I reached over the bed toward the poster. What if one of those sharp green pincers shot out and grabbed me?

I tugged all four thumbtacks out as fast as I could. Then I grabbed the poster and rolled it up—tight.

Whew! Getting it off the wall felt good. I put my Shaq poster back up and felt even better. Maybe everything would turn back to normal now.

I decided to put the poster in my closet. I stuck it behind one of my failures—the hula hoop. The twins were hula hoop champions—of course. I could never get that thing to stay up.

But I didn't fail with the poster, I reminded myself. I could claim the prize from the poster company. I'd won it fair and square. For once, I'd beaten the twin monsters of Fear Street!

I rummaged around in my top desk drawer and found a postcard. "It's a mantis," I wrote on the card. Then I addressed it to the poster company. I printed my name and address in one corner and stuck a stamp on the other.

I decided to mail the postcard right away. I jumped down the stairs two at a time, told my parents I'd be right back, and jogged to the mailbox on the corner.

As I dropped the postcard in, I breathed a sigh of relief. I'd solved the Mystery Stereogram and mailed in the answer. I was finished with the poster. I felt great!

I glanced over at the twins' house as I walked

back home. I couldn't wait to see their faces when my prize arrived.

I imagined their reaction again and again as I climbed the stairs to my room. I could hear their angry little squeals. I could see their faces getting all red and scrunched up.

I sat down to do my homework, and before I knew it, it was time for bed. I was so tired! What a day!

I placed my glasses on the small table next to my bed. Then I punched my pillow a few times and turned off the bedside light. I wanted to dream about the moment the twins realized I'd beaten them.

But I couldn't fall asleep.

What was that strange light?

I sat up and glanced around.

I saw a faint glow. It came from under the closet door.

Did I leave the light on in my closet when I put the poster away?

I threw back the covers to hop out of bed. But I stopped when I saw the crack under the door begin to glow brighter and brighter.

With my eyes trained on the strange glow, I reached back, fumbled for the lamp switch—and sent the lamp crashing to the floor. The lightbulb shattered into a million razor-sharp pieces.

I quickly turned back to the closet door—and gasped!

A few bright fluorescent dots floated out from beneath it.

They shimmered like lightning bugs. Green, pink, orange, and yellow lightning bugs. They circled slowly, chasing one another.

Huh? Am I seeing things? I wondered. I knelt on the edge of my bed. Were my eyes playing tricks on me the way Dad thought? Had I fooled around with 3-D too much?

More dots floated out. More and more and more. Thousands of the dots streamed from under the closet door.

They bounced off the walls.

Careened off the furniture.

They swirled in lazy circles.

I gaped at them, frozen in horror. In disbelief.

Swirling. Swirling.

And then, without warning, they started swirling around me!

And buzzing—an angry, grating buzz—the sound of a thousand hungry insects!

7

I pressed my hands against my ears as hard as I could, but I couldn't keep the noise out. I felt as if the buzzing dots were trapped inside my head. Crawling through my ears and behind my eyes.

The dots glowed brighter. They twirled around me faster and faster.

My eyes itched and burned. I wanted to rub them, but I was afraid to unblock my ears.

The itching spread through my entire body. Down my neck, my chest, around my back, over my arms and legs.

I squeezed into the corner of my bed. Then I quickly grabbed for my pillow and pulled it over my head.

I wanted to scream for help, but I was afraid to open my mouth. I was afraid the dots would fly inside me. Crawl down my throat and into my stomach.

A foul odor rose over my room. I could smell it through the pillow. Worse than a skunk or rotten eggs or spoiled milk.

My stomach lurched. My throat and nose burned. My entire body itched.

I had to do something!

I had to stop the swirling dots!

I released my grip on the pillow and grabbed my bedspread. I wound it around my arm. Then I dropped to my hands and knees and crawled toward the closet.

The buzzing grew almost unbearable without the pillow protecting my ears.

I forced myself to inch forward—until I reached the closet. The dots were still spilling out.

I shoved one edge of the blanket under the door. The dots kept coming. My fingers shook as I stuffed more of the blanket into the crack. I could feel the dots pushing against it. Struggling to get out.

I kept jamming the blanket under the door until it was wedged in tight. Then I backed up.

No light leaked from the closet.

I spun around.

All the dots in the room had disappeared.

I sat down carefully on the edge of my bed. I stared at the closet door. Waiting to see if the dots could escape my barricade.

I stared into the darkness for a long time. The room remained dark and silent.

The knots in my stomach disappeared. My hands fell open at my sides. I realized I'd been clenching my teeth, and I relaxed my jaws.

My breathing came slower and deeper. My eyes began drifting closed. I couldn't stay awake any longer. I crawled back under the covers and shut my eyes.

I flopped over onto my stomach—my favorite sleeping position. . . .

Crack!

The noise jerked me wide awake. It sounded like a tree being split by lightning.

Crack! There it was again.

41

The room was still dark, but I knew where the noise was coming from. The closet.

I crept slowly across the bed. My eyes locked on the closet door.

"No!" I cried as my eyes adjusted to the darkness. "This can't be!"

The door was bulging—bulging out into the room. The wood stretching and stretching—like a balloon about to pop.

Then I heard a *whooshing* sound. And the door seemed to suck itself back in.

Then it began to swell again. Pushing its way farther and farther into the room. The wood groaned and cracked. I could hear it splintering under the strain.

In and out.

In and out.

Every time the door swelled, the wood cracked some more.

The door was splitting open. Splitting right in two.

And then I spied it.

Jutting out through the split in the door.

A giant feeler.

8

"Helllp!" I screamed as I dived across my bed. I grabbed my glasses and shoved them on.

"Wes! Wes! What's wrong?" Mom stumbled into my room in her polka-dot nightgown and matching slippers.

She switched on the overhead light and sat down on my bed next to me. "Did you have a nightmare?" she asked, wrapping her arms around my shaking shoulders.

"No," I croaked. My tongue felt like cotton and I couldn't stop my teeth from chattering. "It's—

it's the m-m-mantis. He's trying to break out of the closet. He—"

Mom gave the closet a quick glance. "Slow down a minute, Wesley," she said, smoothing out my rumpled hair. "Take a deep breath and calm down."

I took a deep breath.

"Now, what did you say was in the closet?"

"The praying mantis. I tried to tell you at dinner," I said. "That's what was hidden in the Mystery Stereogram. You know, the one I got from Sal's Five-and-Ten?"

Mom gave a hesitant nod.

"Well, it's alive. And it can get out of the poster."

Mom rolled her eyes.

"You've got to believe me," I pleaded. "The mantis ate a moth that landed on the poster. And Fluffums."

"It ate Fluffums?" Mom exclaimed.

"No, no. The mantis pulled that clump of fur out of him. That's why I put the poster away in my closet. It's dangerous. It's really dangerous. And now the mantis almost smashed through the closet door."

Mom stared hard at the closet door again, then

44

peered around my room. My lamp lay on the floor with the shade knocked off. Pieces of the broken lightbulb were scattered everywhere. And my bedspread was stuffed under the closet door.

"I think we should open the closet and look inside, Wes," Mom said, patting my shoulder.

"I d-don't think that's a good idea, Mom," I stammered.

"Now, come on, Wes," she crooned. "We'll open up the closet door, and you'll see—everything will be fine. Just fine."

I forced myself over to the closet, tiptoeing around the pieces of broken glass. I examined the door closely. It seemed okay.

I rubbed my hand over the wood.

Smooth. No cracks. Not even a splinter.

Mom padded up beside me. "Now," she said patiently, "open the door."

I hesitated for a second. Yes, I decided. Mom was right. I had to open the closet. I had to know if the mantis was still waiting for me.

I slowly pulled the bedspread out from under the door.

My eyes were glued to the crack at the bottom.

No light. No dots. No buzzing sound. Safe so far.

Mom reached over my shoulder and turned the doorknob. A cold chill ran down my spine. Huge drops of perspiration dripped from my forehead. My pajamas began to stick to me.

"Hmmm. It seems to be stuck," Mom said. She twisted the doorknob both ways and pulled harder.

"No! Don't!" I shouted. I grabbed her wrist.

"Your hands are like ice cubes!" she exclaimed.

"I'm scared!" I admitted, gripping her arm tighter. "Maybe the mantis doesn't want us to get in. Maybe it's holding the door shut."

Mom gave me a quick hug. "It's okay," she said softly. "These old wooden doors just get sticky sometimes."

She tried the doorknob again. This time it turned.

My temples pounded. My pulse began to race. I held my breath as she slowly opened the door.

But I didn't look inside. I couldn't. I just studied her face. Waited for her reaction. But her expression didn't change.

She reached into the closet. Pulled on the chain that switches on the closet light. "Seems to be okay," she said. Then she stepped back so I could see inside.

My heart hammered in my chest as I pushed up my glasses to peer into the closet.

Everything seemed—normal.

Just as I'd left it.

The poster still lay behind the hula hoop—still tightly rolled up.

I shoved a couple of shirts aside. Nothing behind them.

I studied the lightbulb in the closet ceiling. Normal.

I felt the inside of the door. No cracks.

A sigh escaped my lips.

I shuffled over to my bed and collapsed into it. My arms and legs had turned to limp noodles. "Maybe it *was* a nightmare," I mumbled.

"They can feel awfully real," Mom answered. She picked up my lamp and returned it to the nightstand. "I'll be right back. I want to sweep up that broken glass before you cut your feet."

As soon as Mom left, I bolted over to the closet door and stuffed the bedspread back into the crack. This wasn't a dream. This was real. And I wasn't taking any chances.

When I heard Mom's slippers clomping back toward my room, I leaped back in bed. She handed me a new lightbulb, and I screwed it into my lamp right away. She didn't ask me about the bedspread—even though I know she noticed it shoved back under the door.

Mom swept the bulb pieces into a dustpan and emptied them into my wastebasket. "Should I switch this off, Wes?" She pointed to the overhead light.

"That's okay, Mom. I'll get it."

"Good night, Wes," she said. "Call me if you need me."

"Good night."

"Good night. What a joke, I thought. This was the worst night of my life. And it wasn't over yet.

I felt okay with Mom in the room. But as soon as she left, I couldn't stop staring at the closet. Waiting for something to happen. Something bad.

I thought maybe I should take the poster out to the garbage. But then I imagined the mantis escaping from the poster, bursting through the front door, and crawling up here to strangle me in my sleep.

No. Taking it outside wouldn't help.

I decided to bring the poster to school tomorrow and show it to Mr. Gosling. He's a scientist. Kind of. Maybe he'd have a logical explanation.

I left on all the lights. I propped the pillows

against the headboard so I could watch the closet. And just to be extra safe, I left my glasses on. Now I'd be ready to run if the dots came back.

Would they come floating out again?

Would they?

I vowed to stay up all night to find out.

9

Bzzzz. Bzzzz. Bzzzzz.

The dots are back!

I leaped out of bed and charged out of my room. I stood in the empty hallway, trying to catch my breath. My chest heaved up and down. I started to wheeze.

Bzzzzz. Bzzzzz. Bzzzzz.

Wait a minute. I knew that sound.

I stood up against the doorframe and peeked into my room.

No dots.

My alarm clock—ringing. Only my alarm.

I hurried back into my room and shut off the clock. Then I checked out my room.

The lights were still on.

My bedspread was still stuffed under the closet door.

I had made it through the night. Somehow.

I felt so relieved—until I realized I couldn't get dressed without opening the closet to get my clothes.

I crept over to the closet door and pressed my ear against it. No sounds. No insects buzzing.

I knelt and slid the bedspread out from under the crack. Then I opened the closet with a quick jerk.

No mantis!

I grabbed a pair of jeans and my red flannel shirt and pulled them on. I stuffed my feet into my socks and high-tops. Then I lifted the poster with two fingers. The paper felt damp and sort of sticky. I slid it into my backpack and raced downstairs.

I couldn't wait to talk to Mr. Gosling. He knew all about optics. He had a scientist's mind. He'd help me figure this out.

"You okay this morning?" Dad asked. He began slicing a banana over his cornflakes.

"Uh—sure," I answered. I shook some cereal into a bowl and splashed on some milk. "Just a bad dream," I added. I didn't want to talk to my parents about the mantis again until I figured out what was going on.

I wolfed down the cereal and chugged a glass of apple juice. "Got to go," I called. I slipped my backpack on and headed for the door.

Clawd wound himself around my legs. I bent over to pet him, and the poster started to slide out of my backpack. "Yeooww!" Clawd tore away from me like a streak of lightning.

I sighed. "Bye," I called again and left. I had to get some answers today.

As I walked to school, I kept reaching back and touching the poster. Making sure it was still there. I felt as if I had some sort of monster trapped in a bottle. And I didn't want it to get loose.

I felt extra glad when I spotted Lauren waiting for me at our usual corner. She was wearing a bright blue jacket that matched her eyes. And she had her black hair pulled back with a matching headband.

Lauren frowned as I jogged up to her. "Hey, Wes, you look wrecked. Are you okay?"

"Not really," I admitted. I reached back and touched the poster again.

We turned onto Hawthorne Street, and I told Lauren about everything. The mantis. The moth. Clawd, Fluffums, the real, live nightmare in my bedroom last night. And my plan to ask Mr. Gosling for help. I talked nonstop.

When I finally finished, we were a block away from school. "Well, what do you think?"

"Uh," Lauren started. She chewed her lip for a minute. "Wes, this isn't a joke or anything, is it?" she asked. "I mean, is this a story you're just trying out on me? Before you tell it to the twins?"

"Of course not!" I protested. "I wouldn't joke about something like this. It's too weird. Besides, why would I try to fool you?"

"Okay, okay." Lauren held her hand up. "But you have to admit—it is a really strange story."

"I know. But you *do* believe me, don't you?"

"Sure," Lauren said. But I could tell she really wasn't sure. "Talking to Mr. Gosling is a good idea," Lauren continued. "He's logical and all. Maybe he can figure it out. Anyway, whatever happens, Wes, remember—you beat the twins!"

"Yeah. I did. I almost forgot." We laughed and slapped each other a high five.

Then Lauren's face turned serious. "You know—maybe that creepy guy in the five-and-ten was right. Remember, he kept saying, 'You have the power to see.' Maybe it has something to do with that."

Lauren was really starting to believe me!

We crossed the street. A lot of kids were already hanging around outside the school.

"Hey, there's Kim." Lauren pointed to a red-haired girl wearing bright green leggings and a matching jacket. "I have to borrow her history notes. See you later," she called as she ran ahead. "And be careful!"

"See you later," I called, turning up the cobblestone walkway alone.

I reached back one more time to touch the poster—and something yanked me hard from behind. I stumbled backward.

I tried to turn. But it held both my arms in a tight grip.

I tried to scream. But no words came out.

I struggled to escape, but the more I twisted, the tighter it clung to me. Tighter, tighter. Hauling me right off the sidewalk.

I felt something sharp dig into my neck. Something sharp—like pincers.

10

~~~

"**H**elp!" The word exploded from my throat. "Somebody help me!" I twisted and fought to get free.

And then the thing released me.

I thudded to the ground—and spun around.

The "thing" had four arms. And four legs. And tails growing out of the sides of two ugly snorting heads.

Corny and Gabby.

I sighed and pushed myself to my feet. I felt like a total jerk.

They stared at me, giggling and snorting. "Got you, huh?" Corny taunted.

"Yeah," I shot out. "You're a riot. A real riot. Corny."

"Don't call me that!" Corny scowled.

"Yeah, don't call her that," Gabby echoed, twirling her ponytail.

"Your family owes our family money," Corny announced. "Money for the vet bills our parents had to pay." She narrowed her eyes.

"Lots of money." Gabby sneered.

"And that's not all," Corny jumped in. "The police are going to take your vicious cat away, too."

I could feel my face grow red-hot. I wanted to lunge for the twins and yank them around by their stupid ponytails. "No way! *Your* dog ran into *our* house," I insisted.

At least I beat them at the contest, I thought. And the second my prize arrives, I will rub it in their faces. I will never let them live it down.

But for now I would have to follow Lauren's advice—and ignore them.

Without another word I adjusted my backpack, turned, and left.

* * *

I met Lauren at the lockers right before science. I'd gotten through the first couple of hours of school with no problems. I told her what the twins said that morning about the police taking Clawd away.

"They're making it up. They're such jerks," she said, slamming her locker shut with an extra-loud bang.

I shoved my math book into my locker and hung my jacket on the hook. Then, very carefully, I inched the poster out of my backpack. "I'm going to try and catch Mr. Gosling before class starts."

"Good idea," Lauren agreed.

I turned to go—and a hand reached out from nowhere and snatched my glasses off.

I spun around and dropped the poster. It unrolled on the floor.

"Hey! I can't see!" I yelled. "Give me my glasses back!"

The twins! Those jerks! They had my glasses. They always steal my glasses. They know I can't see without them.

I can't wait to teach those twins a lesson, I fumed.

I heard the twins snorting and giggling all the way up the stairs. They were in Mr. Gosling's class, too. I'd get my glasses back then. But first, I had to find Mr. Gosling.

"Come on, Wes," Lauren interrupted my thoughts. "The bell's about to ring."

I squatted down next to the poster. I wanted to roll it up right away. It felt safer that way.

I tried not to peer directly at the poster. It still scared me—a lot. Instead, I glanced at the tile floor next to the poster. But my eyes were drawn to the colored dots as I rolled it up.

I glanced at it for only a second. But that's all it took.

There it stood.

The mantis.

Staring back at me—with its huge, wet, shiny eyes.

I jumped back in horror and screamed, "It's back! It's back!" I couldn't stop screaming. "It's back!"

"Wes! Wes! What's wrong?" Lauren cried.

I couldn't answer. I could only stare. Stare at the mantis as it fought its way out of the poster.

It twisted and strained, like a prehistoric monster trapped in a tar pit. And all the time it watched me. Watched me with those terrifying bug eyes.

Do something. Do something! a voice cried out inside me. But my feet froze to the floor.

I heard Lauren yelling. But she sounded so far away. I was in some kind of trance. The blood pounded in my temples. My heart felt about to burst out of my chest.

DO SOMETHING! the voice screamed in my head.

I grabbed the poster.

My fingers fumbled as I began to roll it up.

I could feel the mantis pushing, pushing against my curled fingers.

I kept rolling up the poster. Faster. Faster.

And then I lost my grip—and the poster sprang open.

"Ahhh!" I yelled as two long back feelers lunged out and dug into my hands.

I dropped the poster.

The feelers waved wildly in the air as it fell. I slammed my foot down to smash them—and missed. The mantis buzzed furiously.

I stomped again. Harder.

One of its long, spindly legs rose out of the poster. And its razor-sharp pincer locked around my ankle.

"Ow!" I howled, shaking my leg wildly. "It's got me! It's got me!"

"What's happening?" Lauren cried. "What's got you?"

She couldn't see it! The mantis had exploded right out of the poster. It was huge! And she still couldn't see it.

It quivered and shook as it freed itself from the paper.

And it began to grow larger. Much larger than the size of the poster!

"Lauren," I gasped. "It's the mantis. It's out of the poster! It's attacking me! And it's huge!"

The mantis reared up on its back legs. It shot out a pincer and gripped my wrist. And squeezed. Squeezed until my hand felt numb. Squeezed until my fingers turned purple.

I clawed at the pincer, trying to tear it off me.

The mantis's legs lashed out. The sharp barbs tore at my shirt. Ripped right through it. My body stung and burned as its pincers pierced my skin.

It continued to grow. Up. Up.

Now it stood as tall as me!

Its enormous, ugly bug face stared into my eyes.

Then its feelers shot through my hair.

61

"Get it off me!" I screamed again and again.

My arms and legs flailed madly as I tried to struggle free. The mantis wrapped its strong, spindly arms around my neck.

Was it trying to choke me?

Where was Lauren? Why wasn't she helping? "Laur—" Her name stuck in my throat as I gasped for air.

I jerked my head up to try to loosen the huge insect's deadly grip.

"Lauren? Where are you?" I choked out. "Lauren? Lauren?"

"Lauren?"

I saw her. Hurrying down the hall.

Leaving me to fight the giant mantis!

"Aaaagggghhh." A gurgling sound escaped my throat as the mantis squeezed tighter. I couldn't breathe. Bursts of color exploded before my eyes.

I flung my head back.

I stumbled through the hall with the mantis clutching my throat.

Then I whirled around and slammed the mantis into the row of lockers. I heard that high-pitched buzz again, and I felt the pincers loosen.

The insect opened its huge jaws. I could see deep into its mouth. I could smell its sour breath. It snapped its jaws shut inches from my face.

I shoved one arm between the creature and my chest and hurled it from my body. It crashed to the floor with a horrible screech.

Then I spotted Lauren. Leaning against the lockers with her arms folded.

"Very convincing, Wes." She smiled. "If I didn't know better, I'd swear you were wrestling with a huge, invisible praying mantis."

She reached out her hand and gave me a playful shove. "We're going to be really late if—"

The mantis lashed out and locked a pincer around Lauren's wrist.

"Owww! Wes!" she screamed. "Something's got me! Get it off!"

I took a deep breath and gave a sort of karate chop to the mantis's long front leg.

The mantis cried out and flew across the hallway.

"W-what happened?" Lauren stammered, rubbing the red, raw spot where the mantis had sunk its pincer.

"The mantis," I whispered. I watched as its big head slowly turned and its enormous eyes scanned

64

the empty hall. "It's still here, but it's not looking at us right now. Wait. I think it sees something down the hall."

I squinted, but I couldn't see very well—things were a total blur without my glasses.

"It's Mr. Gosling!" Lauren cried. "Quick, Wes! Stop him and tell him about the mantis."

Lauren couldn't see the mantis. But at least she really truly believed me now.

Mr. Gosling ambled down the hall balancing a high pile of books under his chin.

He headed straight for us.

And the mantis.

"Look out!" I yelled.

Too late.

The mantis seized his ankle and sank its jaw into it.

Mr. Gosling let out a low moan. His long legs buckled underneath him. He tumbled face-first on the floor and slid down the hall on his stomach. Dragging the mantis behind him.

I snatched up one of the books he dropped— *Fun with Insects*. I stuck it in my back pocket. It might come in handy, I thought.

I grabbed another book and hurled it at the mantis.

Missed!

"Wes, what are you doing?" Lauren whispered.

"Trying to hit the mantis," I said.

I heaved another book at it.

"Darn! Missed again."

"Where is it, Wes?" Lauren asked. "What's it doing?"

I squinted down the hall. Mr. Gosling climbed to his feet. "It had Mr. Gosling by the ankle," I answered. "Now it's lying right behind him."

"I'd like an explanation," Mr. Gosling bellowed as he strode toward us. His baggy gray cardigan flapped behind him. "Why are you throwing those books? And who tripped me?"

I knew this wasn't the time to get Mr. Gosling's theories about the poster. I had to talk fast. "Uh. No one tripped you. At least Lauren and I didn't trip you. But I did throw your books. I'm sorry about that. But I had to—"

"Had to throw books?" Mr. Gosling questioned me, staring over his glasses. "We'll deal with this later. Now, please help me pick them up." He bent over and started gathering his books.

Lauren and I helped. I kept one eye on the mantis the whole time.

"Quick, Lauren," I whispered. "It's coming!"

"Run for it!" she screamed, dropping her pile of books and sprinting down the hall.

Mr. Gosling pushed himself to his feet and patted his tie down. "What is wrong with her? She threw my books on the floor. I really don't understand this behavior. Maybe you'd both better come with me for a serious talk."

"No, please, Mr. Gosling," I begged. "There's a logical explanation for all this. I'm sure there is. But I need you to help me figure it out."

"Figure it out?" Mr. Gosling asked. "You want me to figure out why *you* are misbehaving?"

"Where is it? Is it gone?" Lauren yelled from halfway down the hall, her voice high and squeaky.

"No," I called.

I studied the mantis, trying to decide what it would do next. It had stopped crawling. Now it seemed to be waiting. Almost motionless. Then, very slowly, it rubbed one of its pincers on the top of its head.

Then it took a step toward Mr. Gosling.

"It's getting closer," I warned.

"What's getting closer?" Mr. Gosling demanded.

I swallowed hard.

67

"Tell him!" Lauren urged. "Tell him before it's too late!"

"Too late for what?" he asked. "Class?" He sounded more confused than angry now.

"Um. Yes. Class," I answered. "Let's go." I scooped up the books Lauren had dropped. I grabbed Mr. Gosling's elbow and quickly steered him around the mantis and over to the stairs.

Lauren started to climb up first.

"Wait!" I yelled. "Where's the poster? I have to have the poster!"

"There!" Lauren pointed. "Near the lockers."

I ran down the hall and scooped it off the floor. As I rolled it up, I noticed a large blank space. The space where the mantis had been.

Lauren raced down the hall, tugging my arm. "Come on," she urged, searching the hall for some sign of the creature. "Where is the thing?"

"It's okay," I answered. "It's busy."

Mr. Gosling stood by the staircase rearranging the books in his arms. The mantis crouched nearby. But it wasn't paying any attention to him. It held its two front legs together in front of its huge eyes.

"Busy doing what?" Lauren asked. I could tell she was working to stay calm.

"It's behind Mr. Gosling. Don't worry, it doesn't seem interested in him. It looks as if it's praying or something," I whispered.

Lauren wrenched my arm. "Doesn't that mean it's getting ready to attack?"

12

~~~

Yes!

Lauren was right!

Now I remembered. The mantis had raised its legs in a praying position right before it ate the moth!

"Let's get out of here!" I shouted.

The mantis began rocking back and forth, with its front legs pressed together.

We raced over to Mr. Gosling. I grabbed for his sleeve, yanking him up the steps.

"Be careful, Wes," he warned. "I'm going to

drop these books again. It doesn't matter if we're a few minutes late."

"Don't want to be any later than we already are," I replied.

"That's right," Lauren agreed.

I heard that terrible buzzing sound—like a million angry mosquitoes. Lauren didn't seem to hear it at all. I glanced over my shoulder.

"It's still behind us," I whispered to Lauren as we reached the top of the stairs. "It's crawling up. Following us!"

"Tell him!" she urged.

We had almost reached the science lab. I jumped in front of the door, blocking it. "Mr. Gosling, there's something you have to know. It's about the stereogram. The one the twins brought to class. There's a mantis in it. A praying mantis. And it's not just 3-D. It's actually alive—"

Mr. Gosling pushed past me. "After class," he answered. I could tell he was fed up.

Lauren and I hurried to our seats. She sits in the back of the class. I sit near the front, right next to the twins.

"Give me back my glasses," I ordered them.

"What glasses?" Corny asked.

71

"Yeah, what glasses?" Gabby chimed in.

"*My* glasses, you—"

I heard a horrible scraping sound at the door. It opened a crack and two long black feelers poked inside. They waved back and forth—searching the air. Searching for something.

"Oh, no!" I moaned.

I turned to Lauren. "It's here!" I mouthed.

"Is there something you would like to share with the rest of the class, Wes?" Mr. Gosling asked.

"Umm, I really need to talk to you about the 3-D poster." I glanced at the door. It swung open wider. The mantis's huge head appeared. Its jaws dripped saliva. "Someone might get hurt if—"

"I told you—we will talk about the poster after class," Mr. Gosling said sternly. Then he began to make his way over to the door.

I wanted to cover my eyes with my hands. Or disappear under my desk. But I knew I had to warn Mr. Gosling. I jumped up from my seat—but I wasn't fast enough.

Mr. Gosling reached the door and—shut it hard, smashing one of the mantis's back legs.

Phew. That was a close one.

The mantis's leg re-formed itself. The buzzing

72

grew louder than ever. I could feel it vibrating through my body. My ears pounded. I covered them with my hands, trying to block out the hideous noise.

"But after class will be too late—" I tried to warn Mr. Gosling.

"After class!" Mr. Gosling exclaimed. "And please don't cover your ears when I'm speaking to you."

The twins started to snort.

I thought my eardrums were going to explode.

"Yes!" I shouted. "I hear you."

"Why are you shouting? What's wrong with you today, Wes?" Mr. Gosling asked. "Are you sick?"

"No," I muttered. I wished I could tell him yes. Then he would send me down to the nurse. The nurse would call my mom. And my mom would come and take me home.

But it was too late for that.

I bought the poster.

I ignored Sal's warnings.

And now I was the only one who could see the mantis. I was the only one who could hear the buzzing. So I had to stay. I had to stop the mantis. If I could.

73

"Let's continue our study of the eye," Mr. Gosling started.

The buzzing slowly faded, but the mantis remained perched by the door. Mr. Gosling began pacing back and forth in front of the classroom—the way he always does. His hands shoved deep into his pockets.

The mantis crept up behind him and followed him—back and forth across the room. Back and forth. It paused when Mr. Gosling paused. It turned when Mr. Gosling turned.

I wanted to scream.

At least it's not praying, I thought. But the mantis definitely had its eye on Mr. Gosling.

Mr. Gosling turned to the chalkboard and drew a side view of the human eye. The mantis reached out to take a swipe at him.

It missed.

I let out a loud gasp.

Mr. Gosling glared at me. Then he turned back to his drawing.

The mantis tried again.

This time its pincer hit the chalkboard.

Screeeech.

Everybody cried out. A few kids held their

hands over their ears. Mr. Gosling glared at me again. As if it were my fault!

At first I was surprised that everyone could hear the *screech*. Then I remembered that other people couldn't see the mantis or hear it buzzing—but they could feel it grab them. So I guess it made sense that they could hear its pincer scraping the chalkboard.

Mr. Gosling slammed the chalk in the rack and marched over to a corner of the room—where his favorite specimen stood under a white sheet.

"Okay," he announced, whipping the sheet off. A human skeleton hung from a stand. It was a little shorter than Mr. Gosling. "We're going to examine the skull today."

The mantis inched over to the skeleton. Its feelers were waving all over the place. It tilted its enormous head, staring hard at the bones. Saliva dripped from it jaws and puddled at its feet. It was hungry, I realized.

I was so nervous, I fumbled with my ruler and it crashed to the floor.

Mr. Gosling ignored me. He rolled the skeleton closer to the class. "Have a look at the bones around your eyes."

"Ooh, gross!" Gabby cried.

Everybody laughed.

The mantis leaned forward and seemed to be sniffing the skeleton. I leaned forward, too. My stomach heaved.

The mantis caught the skeleton's hand between its gaping jaws. It started chewing the finger bones.

The whole class gasped. "Cool trick!" someone yelled.

"I think it's hungry," I mouthed to Lauren.

Mr. Gosling stared at the arm. It looked as if it were waving to us.

"Who's doing that?" Mr. Gosling demanded. "Wes?"

"No!" I protested. "But you have to listen to me. I think it's *really* dangerous now. I think it's hungry."

"What's hungry?" Gabby asked. "The skeleton?"

A few kids laughed.

"It sure looks thin," Corny added.

More laughter.

The mantis grabbed one of the skeleton's legs and started gnawing on the knee.

"What's it doing now?" Gabby called.

"I think it's the cancan," Corny cracked.

The class went completely out of control. They thought the whole thing was a big joke.

Mr. Gosling grabbed the stand and wheeled the skeleton away from the mantis. "This is not a toy," he declared. "I want an apology from the person responsible."

The room fell silent. Except for the sounds coming from the mantis—buzzing and snapping its pincers recklessly in the air. "Don't move the skeleton!" I cried. "You're making it angry!"

The class exploded into laughter.

Mr. Gosling strode over to my desk. He glared down at me. "If I hear one more outburst, you are out of here. Do you understand that?" he growled. "And I don't mean detention. I mean suspension. From school!"

What could I say?

I felt so helpless. I needed to explain everything to Mr. Gosling. To get him on my side.

I placed my head in my hands. Think, Wes. Think.

Then I jerked my head up. Where was the mantis? I'd lost track of him.

77

Oh, no! I slid down in my seat.

The creature had discovered the corner in the back of the room where we kept the class animals.

I thought of the moth.

I remembered Fluffums and the clump of hair.

And I watched in horror as the creature reached its pincer out to the hamster cage.

I stared in horror as it pulled the bars of the hamster cage apart.

I closed my eyes for a moment. Trying to come up with a plan. But a terrifying picture crowded my mind. I saw the mantis shove the hamster into its waiting, dripping jaws—and swallowing it whole. I imagined it moving on to the guinea pigs, the white mice, and the baby frogs.

Here goes, I thought. I'll probably be expelled from school—but I had to take action.

I climbed up on my lab stool. "Free the animals!" I shouted to Lauren. At least that way maybe they wouldn't be sitting targets. Maybe they could run and hide.

Lauren jumped up and ran to the frog aquarium. She scooped up the frogs, two and three at a time, and plunked them on the floor.

They sat there frozen.

The mantis plodded toward them.

They slowly lifted their little heads in the air. They seemed to be sniffing. Then they started hopping in all directions.

Some of the kids began to scream and climb on top of their desks. Most of the kids were laughing.

"Stop that this instant!" I could barely make out Mr. Gosling's voice above the noise.

Lauren ignored him and moved on to the next cage.

"Free them all!" I shouted. I ran to the chalkboard and grabbed the wooden pointer.

"What do you think you're doing?" Mr. Gosling demanded. He grabbed my shoulder and shook it hard.

"Look out!" I yelled as I broke free from his grasp. I charged over to the animal cages, waving the pointer like a sword.

The mantis stood over a cage full of fat white mice. Drooling and praying.

Rocking back and forth.

The mice squeaked wildly, jumping up and down like pieces of popping popcorn.

I made my way carefully to the mantis. The pointer kept slipping from my sweaty palm. I crept up behind the creature and jabbed its side. It spun around and yanked the stick right out of my hand—but it backed off a few feet, buzzing furiously.

I knocked the mice cage over and urged the mice out.

"What are you doing with those mice?" Mr. Gosling exclaimed, throwing his hands up in the air.

"I'm saving their lives!" I answered, clapping loudly so they would scatter.

"What about the turtles?" Jimmy Peterson called out. Everyone was getting into it now.

"Let them go, too!" I commanded. And he did.

The turtles wouldn't move—no matter how much anyone yelled at them. A few kids picked them up so they wouldn't get squashed.

Someone let the garter snake go. The mantis lunged for it. But the snake wriggled under the radiator in a flash. The mantis sent a pincer out, but it couldn't reach.

81

"Good!" I shouted. Now I turned to the bat's cage.

"Not my bat!" Mr. Gosling pleaded, clutching his chest.

The bat was Mr. Gosling's favorite class pet. He found it on a hiking trip. Its wing was broken and Mr. Gosling nursed it back to health. Mr. Gosling would want me to set the bat free if he could see the mantis, I convinced myself.

I flung the black cover off the cage and pulled open the door. The mantis lumbered in our direction. The bat didn't move. It hung from its branch, all wrapped up in its wings.

"It's asleep!" I yelled to Lauren. "And the mantis is headed right for it!"

"Tickle it!" she called.

I brushed it lightly on its underside with my finger. That did it. The bat woke up and burst through the door, excited to be free.

"Get him! Get him!" Mr. Gosling yelled, chasing after the bat.

Someone opened the door to let the mice out, and the bat escaped into the hallway.

Mr. Gosling ran out the door and slammed it behind him.

Suddenly the classroom went quiet. The kids

stopped shouting. All the animals had found hiding places.

It felt creepy.

"Where is it now?" Lauren whispered.

"It's n-not near us," I stammered. "It's poking around Corny's desk."

"Hey! Who knocked my microscope over?" Corny whined. She hurried back to her desk. Gabby was right behind her. But the mantis was no longer there. It had moved on.

What would it do next? I wondered.

"Ooh, my notes are all wet," Gabby complained. "And slimy." She picked them up by the corner.

"Mantis drool," I whispered to Lauren.

"Where is it now?" she asked.

"It's—it's coming this way."

I spotted the pointer on the floor. I snatched it up and crouched under one of the lab tables. My knees trembled and my hands shook.

"What are you going to do?" Lauren asked. She crouched beside me.

"I'm—I'm going to try to stab it with the pointer," I said, inching toward the mantis. I could see its thin green legs as it wobbled down one row and up another.

My pulse started to race as it crawled closer and

closer. A few more feet—and I'd be able to reach it.

Then the bell rang.

"Lunch!" someone shouted.

The kids gathered up their stuff and stampeded out the door. The mantis joined the crowd.

"Where is it now?" Lauren demanded.

"It's—it's gone," I answered.

"Great!" Lauren cheered.

"There's just one problem." I sighed.

"What?" Lauren asked.

"It's headed for the cafeteria."

14

"**D**on't go!" Lauren shouted as I ran out the classroom door. "Don't go without this!" She waved the poster in the air.

I grabbed it. Then we scrambled down the stairs and raced to the cafeteria. Just as we reached the entrance, Lauren skidded to a stop and seized my arm. "What's that noise?"

We both listened.

My stomach churned. "Screaming."

We raced inside. I was certain the mantis had attacked someone.

An apple whizzed by my head.

"Food fight!" someone shrieked.

Food fight? They were screaming about a food fight?

My eyes darted around the cafeteria, searching for the creature. "I see it," I whispered to Lauren. "It's wandering from table to table. And it's drooling like crazy."

"Who took my Twinkie?" a skinny, freckle-faced kid shouted.

"Who stole my peanut-butter-and-banana sandwich?" another kid yelled.

I watched the mantis grab a tub of cottage cheese and scoop up a big glob with its pincer. No one even noticed the tub hovering in the air. There was too much food flying around.

The mantis shoved a ball of the cottage cheese in its mouth—and spit it right back out. It flicked a chunk of it right into the lunchroom teacher's gray hair. Then it began to whip its pincer back and forth with fury, spattering white dots of cottage cheese everywhere.

"Yuck! Who's throwing this stuff?" a kid in a Dodgers baseball cap complained. "It's disgusting." He scraped it off his blue shirt and slung it at someone else.

"Is the mantis doing all this?" Lauren asked.

"Most of it," I answered. "I can't see too well. Corny still has my glasses." I can't wait till I get my hands on her, I muttered to myself.

"What is it doing right now?" she asked.

"It's weird, Lauren," I said as I squinted at it. "Its snatching food and sniffing it—and flinging it away. It isn't eating anything."

"Maybe it's not hungry," Lauren replied.

I shook my head. "It's hungry all right. It's dripping pools of drool. I just don't get it."

Suddenly I remembered the *Fun with Insects* book. I yanked it out of my back pocket. I flipped to the praying mantis page.

"Uh-oh," I moaned.

Lauren tried to read over my shoulder. "What, Wes? What?"

I took a deep breath. "According to this book, the mantis prefers its food alive."

"Alive?" Lauren's huge blue eyes grew wide. "As in walking, breathing alive?"

"Uh-huh."

PLOP. A big glob of carrots landed on my sneaker. Well, at least it doesn't have a cow eye in it, I thought as we both stared down at it—the way the carrots did yesterday. I wished that day had never happened. Because that was the day I first saw the twins' Mystery Stereogram.

Why couldn't I see the mantis that day? I wondered. How come I could see it now? What was different? What—

"What's it doing now? What's it doing now?" Lauren interrupted my thoughts.

I searched the room. It was way in the back of the cafeteria. At that distance I couldn't see it at all.

CRASH!

A huge crash from the back. Followed by a long, terrifying scream.

"What's happening, Lauren? I can't see!"

"A table flipped over by itself!" Lauren yelled.

"I doubt it." We raced to the back of the cafeteria.

I really wish I had my glasses, I thought. "My glasses! That's it!" I shouted.

"What's going on?" Lauren asked the kids gathered around the upside-down table.

"Cornelia is trapped under there," a girl in a bright purple T-shirt answered.

"Yeah," Chad Miller added. "I tried to pull it off

88

her—but something cut me." He held up his hand. A deep jagged scratch ran across the back. "I couldn't see what it was. It was like—invisible or something." Chad shook his head, confused.

Lauren and I pushed through the crowd of kids—and there was Corny. Her legs were pinned under part of the table. But that wasn't what was holding her down. The mantis was draped across her chest!

Her hands thrashed the air as she screamed, "Get it off me!"

"Lauren! It's sitting on Corny. I have to get my glasses from her!"

"I know she's a total jerk. But shouldn't we help her before we worry about the glasses?" Lauren protested.

"No! I mean yes . . . I mean . . . the first time I saw the poster, I had my glasses on and everything was okay," I quickly explained. "But when I look at it without my glasses . . . I make it come alive. I think."

I stared down at Corny to check the mantis. A long strand of drool stretched from its mouth to the floor. And it was rubbing its front legs together—praying.

I shoved some kids aside and knelt next to Corny. The mantis started to rock back and forth.

"Give me my glasses," I ordered.

"First get me out of here," Corny screeched. "Something's on top of me! But I can't see it!"

I stared at her hard. "If you want to get out of here alive, give me my glasses. Now!"

Corny's face grew pale. The mantis was rocking. Rocking back and forth. Corny's eyes darted frantically to see what was pressing against her.

The mantis raised its pincers.

It opened its huge, gaping jaw.

A thick wad of drool oozed out on Corny's arm.

Corny screamed.

"Now!" I yelled at her. "Now!"

"Here!" She slid my glasses out of her pocket.

I leaped up and shoved them on. I had only seconds before the mantis would strike.

I concentrated on the mantis.

Nothing happened.

"Is it working, Wes?" Lauren whispered.

"Ssh," I said. "I have to concentrate." Beads of sweat dripped down my face as I focused.

The mantis moved slightly. It was crouching.

Getting ready to spring.

To lunge for Corny's neck.

I stared as hard as I could.

My head ached.

My eyes throbbed and burned.

I wanted to close them. I needed to close them.

My eyelids started to drop—and then it happened.

Tiny dots began to appear. Hundreds of them. Thousands of them. Orange, green, pink, and yellow. Fluorescent dots all over the mantis's body.

They began to glow. Brighter and brighter.

Don't blink. Don't blink, I chanted to myself.

The dots began to swarm. They swirled and raced up and down the mantis's legs. All the way up its body. Up to its feelers. Up to its head.

Then the dots whirled apart. It was like watching an explosion in slow motion.

The dots flooded the cafeteria. Bouncing off the tables. The chairs. The kids. Buzzing. Buzzing.

And then they were gone.

Corny wiggled out from under the table. "Thanks for nothing, Wes," she muttered.

"Did it work?" Lauren asked softly.

I unrolled the poster clutched in my hand.
The blank space was—gone.
I breathed out the longest sigh of my life.
"It's back in the poster, Lauren."
"Yes! You were right!" she cried. "We're safe!"
"Not yet," I corrected her. "We're not safe until we destroy this poster for good."

15

"The scissors are in the top drawer, next to the refrigerator," I told Lauren. We had a long talk when we got home from school about the best way to get rid of the mantis. This was all we could think of.

"Are you sure it's safe?" Lauren asked.

"I hope so," I said.

I read a note stuck to the refrigerator. "Mom says she and Dad took Vicky shopping. So this is the best time."

I made certain my glasses were firmly in place. Then I rolled the poster out on the kitchen table.

Lauren handed me the scissors.

I laughed nervously. "My hands are shaking."

I swallowed hard. "Here goes." I turned the poster from side to side, trying to decide where to cut. Actually I was stalling. I didn't know what would happen if I cut the poster. Would the mantis burst out if I sliced through the dots?

I squeezed my eyes shut and snipped into the paper. I did it really quickly. I was scared.

No buzzing.

I opened my eyes and snipped again. This time I cut the poster in half.

"Think it worked?" Lauren asked.

I stared down at the two pieces. "I don't know."

"Are you going to make sure?" she asked.

I nodded. "I guess I have to."

"Be careful. Have your glasses ready," Lauren warned.

My stomach clenched. "I will." I slid my glasses down my nose. Then I peeked over the top of them at the left half of the poster.

I jerked my head away and shoved my glasses up. "It's still there," I groaned.

"Okay, okay," Lauren said. "Let's stay calm." But she didn't sound calm. "Maybe we just need to cut it in smaller pieces."

Lauren picked up the scissors. "I'll do it this time." She made a tiny cut, then glanced over at me. "Turn around, okay? It makes me nervous when you stare at the poster—even with your glasses on."

I turned away from the kitchen table.

Snip. Snip. Snip. I grew more and more nervous with each little snip.

I heard Lauren slam the scissors down on the table. Then I heard a tearing sound.

"What are you doing?" I asked.

"I'm ripping it up. It's quicker than the scissors," she explained.

Riiiip. I hated that sound even more than the scissor snips. A drop of sweat rolled down my cheek. I wiped my clammy hands on my jeans.

I heard Lauren rip the paper again and again and again.

What if it's still there?

What if we're only making things worse?

What if we're making the mantis *angry?*

"That ought to do it," she announced. "You can turn around now."

I whirled to face her—and gasped. A mound of paper filled the center of the table. Tiny pieces about the size of the fingernail on my pinky.

Lauren's face flushed pink. "I didn't want to take any chances."

"I guess I should check it again," I said. I hoped she would say I didn't have to.

But she nodded. I knew she was right. We had to be sure the creature was really gone.

I pulled my glasses down to the end of my nose. The pieces were so tiny. I could barely see them.

I leaned over the table.

I still couldn't be sure.

A drop of sweat ran down my chin and plopped onto the pile.

I bent my head lower and lower. Closer and closer.

The blood pounded in my ears.

"Be careful not to—"

Before Lauren could finish her warning, it was too late.

A tiny pincer lashed out at my face.

My glasses went flying.

I heard them hit the floor.

"Lauren! Get my glasses!" I yelled.

"Where did they go?" she cried, searching the floor on her hands and knees.

"I don't know!" I answered. "Hurry!"

Tiny legs burst out of each piece of the poster.
Tiny eyes glared up at me.
Sharp little pincers clicked open and shut.
They swarmed over the table.
Hundreds.
Hundreds of miniature praying mantises!

16

"They're back!"

"Huh? They?" Lauren shrieked.

"They're pouring out of all the pieces!" I cried.

"Oh, no!" Lauren moaned. "What do we do now?"

"We've got to find my glasses!"

"I'm checking under the table," she called.

"Wait!" I yelled. But it was too late.

The mantises marched down the table legs— toward Lauren. The kitchen filled with their horrible buzzing.

I grabbed a dish towel from the counter and whipped it at the little monsters.

"Get out of there! The mantises are headed right for you!"

Lauren scrambled out from under the table. "They're on me! They're on me!" she cried, jumping up and down. "I think they're in my hair!" She leaned forward and slapped at her head.

"Hold still!" I yelled at her. "Let me look!" The buzzing grew louder and louder. I could hardly think.

She shook her head violently. "I can't hold still, Wes. I just can't! Do something! Please!"

I grabbed her head to hold it still. The green insects swarmed over her hair—burrowing deeper and deeper.

I tried to pick them out, but it was impossible. They lashed out with their sharp pincers. "Quick! Go to the sink!"

"Water!" Lauren shouted. "Perfect. We'll drown them."

Then I turned on the cold tap full force and guided Lauren's head under it.

I turned to check the table. "Oh, no!" I spotted a mantis launch off the table and soar into the air. "They can fly."

"It's not working," Lauren called from the sink. "I can feel them. They're starting to bite!"

"No, it is working, Lauren," I said, peering at her head. "I can see them spilling off."

I felt a sharp sting on the back of my neck. Then on my forehead. My nose. One of my ears.

The mantises swarmed around my head.

Dodged at my face.

Clawed into my skin.

I stumbled backward, pawing frantically at my head.

Then I heard a terrifying sound.

And I knew we were doomed.

17

CRUNNCH.

I heard a crunch. Underfoot.

And I knew what I had stepped on. With a sinking feeling I snatched my glasses up from the floor. Maybe only one lens broke, I silently wished. Maybe only one.

Nope.

Both of them—smashed.

Yes. We're both doomed, I thought.

I grabbed the dish towel again. This time I threw it over my head, trying to protect myself from the stinging creatures.

Think, Wes. Think, I ordered myself. They are bugs. How do you get rid of bugs?

I dashed to the wall switch and flicked on the ceiling light.

Yes! The mantises flew toward the light and began to circle. A few bounced off the bulb and dropped to the table. Then they staggered up and launched themselves at the glowing bulb again.

They were under control. For now.

Lauren pulled her head out from under the tap. Water streamed down her long hair. Down her face. "Where are they?"

I pointed to the ceiling light.

Lauren grinned. "Great! Now all we have to do is find your glasses!"

"Uh. I already did," I admitted. I held them up.

"Oh, no! Now what do we do?" Lauren wailed. "Do you have an extra pair?"

"That *was* my extra pair," I answered.

I peered up at the insects, squinting into the light. The buzzing noise suddenly changed to a low humming sound.

My eyes felt itchy, but I kept staring—because I noticed a small change.

"Something's happening," I murmured.

"What?" Lauren grabbed my arm. "What's happening. Tell me!"

"They're changing."

"Changing? How?" Lauren demanded. "They're not growing, are they? Please, don't tell me they're growing."

"No. They're definitely not growing. But they're not getting smaller, either." I blinked several times. "They're turning into those dots. It's just like what happened in the cafeteria!"

"Yes!" Lauren cried. "That means they're disappearing!"

"I don't think so, Lauren."

"Well, what are they doing?" she cried.

"They're still up there. Humming. Orange, pink, yellow, and green humming dots," I explained. "Now they're swirling around the light. Really fast. The colors are almost melting together."

"Maybe they're dying," Lauren suggested.

"No!" I exclaimed. "No! They're forming one big ball of color now! One big ball of green!"

"Oh, n-noooo," Lauren wailed. "Look!"

I ripped my eyes away from the swirling green ball of color.

"Look!" Lauren cried again, pointing to the table with a trembling hand. "The poster," she croaked.

I shifted my gaze to the table.

The pile of tiny paper scraps had vanished.

The poster had grown back—in one whole piece.

With the big white mantis-shaped spot in the middle.

18

I raised my eyes to the green ball.

It fell to the floor with a dull thump.

Two black feelers thrust out of the top.

Six long bristly legs burst out of the back.

The pincers on the front legs snapped open and closed.

"Get out!" I yelled at Lauren. "Get out while you can! The mantis is back!"

"I'm staying!" she shouted. "Where is it? What should I do?"

"It's coming this way. Circle around the table

and stand on the other side of the room. Maybe it won't be able to decide which of us to go for!"

Lauren slid around the table. "What's it doing now? Do you think it's going to attack?"

I backed up until I hit the wall. "It's so close I can't move." I gulped. "It's in a praying position."

"Wes, play dead!" Lauren cried. "It wants to eat food that's still alive!"

I slumped onto the floor and rolled my eyes back in my head. I tried to hold my breath.

For a second nothing happened. Then I felt the mantis's cold feelers probing my neck.

It's trying to decide if I'm alive, I thought. If I move a muscle, it will attack.

I could feel its hot breath on my cheek.

Its saliva drip down my face.

My eyelids twitched as its creepy pincers crawled along my skin.

I wanted to bat it away.

Don't move. Don't move.

I wanted to breathe. My chest felt tight. My lungs were about to burst.

Don't move! Don't move!

Slowly I felt the mantis slide away. I heard him slither in his drool across the kitchen floor.

I opened one eye.

I couldn't spot the mantis. Where was it?

My lungs were definitely going to explode now. I took a tiny breath. Then I opened my other eye and lifted my head slightly off the floor.

Now I could see it.

But Lauren couldn't. She was watching me. Biting her lip. Twisting her hands together. Worrying about me.

And there was the mantis—standing next to her. Standing next to Lauren—who was breathing. Moving. Alive.

I slowly pushed myself off the floor.

"Don't move!" I mouthed.

Lauren understood.

I crept over to the mantis. Slowly. Very slowly.

It was perched next to the stove. Rocking back and forth.

Rubbing its pincers together.

"Hey, what are you guys doing? Why are you crawling on the floor?" a voice called from the doorway.

Vicky.

The mantis snapped its head toward my sister. I grabbed Lauren's arm and pulled her away from the huge insect.

"Wow! Your glasses are ruined," Vicky said,

lifting the broken frames from the table. "Wes, you're in major trouble!"

The mantis's feelers waved with fury. Its eyes darted from me to Lauren to Vicky and back.

"I've never broken my glasses," Vicky bragged. "Never even lost them. Wait until Mom and Dad see." She pushed her glasses up.

I slid along the wall toward her. Then I jumped up, grabbed her glasses off her face, and pushed her away.

"Hey, what are you doing?" she yelled. "Those are mine!"

She tried to snatch them back.

"Ssh!" I warned. I held them high over my head.

She hopped up and down, but she couldn't reach them.

"Vicky, wait outside. I'll give them back in a minute," I promised.

"I'm not leaving without my glasses!" Vicky folded her arms in front of her. "And you'd better not break them!"

I forced her glasses on my face. They were way too small. They pinched my nose. And they didn't quite reach my ears.

"You look stupid," Vicky said.

"Quiet!" I warned. I had to concentrate.

I stared at the mantis.

I moved closer to it and stared really hard.

I strained to see every detail.

Focus. Focus. Don't blink.

I moved in closer.

I stared.

Disappear. Please—disappear back into the poster.

This *has* to work, I told myself. It *has* to.

But the mantis didn't move.

19

"The glasses aren't working!" I moaned. "They're just not working."

The mantis lashed out—so fast I didn't see it coming. But I felt it.

It had me by the neck. Choking off my air.

Its pincers raked my skin.

Its huge eyes gleamed greedily into mine.

Its jaws snapped open and shut. Then it lifted me right off the floor.

Lauren and Vicky gasped as I rose up.

"He's floating!" Vicky cried.

I kicked helplessly.

"Wes, you're scaring me!" Vicky cried.

"Keep staring, Wes! Keep staring!" Lauren yelled.

I gazed directly into the mantis's face. Colors swirled through its deep black eyes. Its eyes looked like two giant kaleidoscopes now. Swirling colors in orange, pink, yellow, green.

Swirling colors!

Colored dots!

"It's working!" I cried. "I think it's working!"

Vicky's glasses *were* working. They were weaker than mine—so they were just taking longer!

Fluorescent dots began to race over the mantis's legs and feelers. Over its whole body!

Then the dots drifted apart.

I crumpled to the floor, but I kept Vicky's glasses pressed against my face.

Dots bounced off the refrigerator. They hit the screen door. They whirled and swirled like mini-tornadoes through the kitchen.

"Give me my glasses back now," Vicky whined. "You're acting crazy."

"Just one more minute, Vicky," I begged. "One more minute." I knew I had almost defeated it.

"Wes! The poster!" Lauren exclaimed, dashing over to the table.

111

I forced myself up and peered over her shoulder.

The white mantis-shaped spot had filled in with color. The mantis was back where he belonged.

Sal had definitely been right. Some things *are* better left in two dimensions.

I collapsed into a kitchen chair.

"We won! We won!" Lauren cheered.

"Not yet." I sighed. "We still have to get rid of the poster."

"Give me my glasses back, Wes." Vicky stomped her feet on the floor.

"Not yet, Vicky," I murmured.

"I'll get Mom and Dad. They'll make you."

"Where are Mom and Dad?" I asked.

"They're outside in the front yard burning a pile of leaves," Vicky replied. Then she ran out, slamming the screen door behind her.

I turned to Lauren and smiled. I eyed the poster. "Let's burn it!"

"Yesss!" Lauren held up her palm and we high-fived.

We dashed out to the front yard. "Hi, Mom!" I called. "Where's Dad?"

"He's in the back, collecting more leaves," she answered. "Wes, what are you doing with your sister's glasses?" Vicky stood beside her—squinting at me triumphantly.

"Uhhh. It's part of a science project," I blurted out.

"For Mr. Gosling's class. Optics," Lauren added.

"Please let me wear them for five more minutes, Vicky," I pleaded.

"Let your brother wear them for a few minutes, Vicky. It's for school."

Vicky dug her foot into the dirt and kicked a chunk of it on my jeans.

"Come on, Vicky," Mom said, wrapping an arm around her shoulder. "Let's help Dad with the leaves in the backyard. Then we'll all go in and have some ice cream."

"Can I throw them into the fire? Can I have chocolate-banana-chunk? Can I give Clawd some?"

"No, yes, and yes," Mom replied as they made their way around back.

I peered up at the sky. It was almost dark. A full orange moon glowed above.

I turned to Lauren. "Okay," I said. "Here goes nothing." I tossed the poster into the center of the fire.

113

The flames caught on the edge of the poster. Then there was a bang—like a firecracker shooting off.

Lauren and I jumped back.

"Guess we're kind of nervous." Lauren giggled nervously. "I don't see anything weird happening. Do you?"

"No," I answered. Then I sniffed the air. It suddenly smelled bad. Really bad. Like the mantis's sour breath.

The fire engulfed the poster now. Furious flames shot through it and licked the sky.

Smoke began to stream from the center of the leaf pile. Greenish-gray smoke. It rose fast—in a long, straight ribbon.

Then I heard the high-pitched buzzing. Louder. Louder. Louder. I wanted to cover my ears. But I had to hold Vicky's glasses on.

Lauren glanced at me. "You okay?" she asked. I nodded.

The smoke drifted higher in the sky. Drifted past the full, bright, orange moon. Then it began to curl.

The smoke curled and curled—into the form of a perfect praying mantis. Huge and dark, it floated in front of the moon.

Then it disappeared.

I turned to Lauren. "Did you see that?" I asked.

"See what?" she said.

"Never mind," I replied.

No one else could see the mantis.

No one else could hear its terrible buzzing.

No one else could make it come alive.

The mantis was my own private nightmare.

A nightmare in 3-D.

And it was over.

Or was it?

20

Two weeks later Lauren came home from school with me. We planned to do some homework together.

"Wes, you got a package today," Mom said when she walked into the kitchen. She set down a cylinder-shaped package on the kitchen table.

Lauren and I exchanged glances.

"The Mystery Prize!" we cried together.

We both dropped our pencils.

I picked the package up. I checked out the return address. "It's from the poster company," I told Lauren. "It's definitely my prize."

"Open it!" Lauren said.

I tore the wrapping off one end and slid the prize out of the cylinder.

"I can't believe it! Another poster!" I said. I rolled it open on the table.

"Oh, no!" Lauren gasped. "Careful, Wes," she said under her breath.

"Another stereogram?" Mom asked, looking over our shoulders. "Is that the prize? Can you see it, Lauren?"

Lauren squinted at the poster. "Uh-uh. I can't see a thing," she said. "Just those black and brown lines."

Mom spent a long time staring at it. But she couldn't make it out, either.

"Hey, what's up? Cool! Whose poster? What is it? Can I have a look?" It was Vicky, of course.

"Sure, have a look," I said, shoving the poster toward her.

"Nope. Can't see a thing. Mom, what's for dinner? Can I have a snack now? Please? Where's Clawd?"

"Pizza. No. In the backyard," Mom told Vicky.

Lauren moved closer. "Are you going to try to see it?" she whispered.

"Do you think I should?" I asked.

117

Lauren shrugged. "Might as well. We know how to control it, don't we?"

I leaned on the table and looked over the top of my glasses.

It took me only a few seconds to see it.

It was big.

And hairy.

And coming straight at me.

A gigantic tarantula scurried out from under a rock and reached a hairy leg right out of the poster.

I jumped backward and nearly fell over Vicky.

"Wes!" Mom cried. "What on earth is wrong with you?"

"Nothing, Mom. It's okay," I replied. I rolled the poster up as fast as I could. "Lauren, can you give me a hand with these books?" I asked.

When we got upstairs, I told her. "There's a monster in the poster. A huge tarantula. And, Lauren," I whispered, "it wants to get out!"

"Come on, Fluffy!" came a voice from next door.

Lauren and I peered out the window.

I saw Gabby. She and Corny were playing with Fluffums. This was the game: They had a stuffed cat, white like Clawd. It had a collar around its

118

neck and a leash. They were dragging the stuffed cat in a circle. They were urging Fluffums to chase it and catch it.

"Come on, Fluff," Corny instructed. "Get that nasty old cat."

Fluffums went running after the cat. He grabbed it and chewed on its neck, growling.

"Good boy!" Gabby cried, patting the dog.

It made me feel sick.

"I'm really starting to dislike that family," Lauren said.

The twins stared up at us. "Hey, where is your cross-eyed cat?" Corny called.

"Yeah, Fluffums wants to play!" Gabby added.

They were both twirling their ponytails and smirking.

I turned to Lauren. "I bet I can make them promise to keep that little hairball away from Clawd from now on."

I leaned out the window. "Hey, you guys, I forgot to tell you!" I shouted. "I won the prize. I solved the Mystery Stereogram."

"Yeah, for sure!" Gabby said, rolling her eyes.

"No way," Corny added.

I sighed and ducked back in the window.

"Bet they'd just love to see my prize," I said. I

tapped the tarantula poster on my hand. "Maybe I'll even give it to them."

"Good idea," Lauren replied, grinning evilly. "I'll hold your glasses this time. You don't want to break another pair."

"Corny! Gabby!" I called out the window. "Wait right there. I have a really cool surprise for you!"

Are you ready for another walk
down Fear Street?
Turn the page for a terrifying
sneak preview.

R·L·STINE'S

GHOSTS OF FEAR STREET ® #5

STAY AWAY FROM THE TREE HOUSE

Coming in mid-January 1996

I was shivering.

But that was a good sign!

Yes. Cold was definitely a good sign.

Because cold spots meant ghosts!

"Do you see anything?" my brother Steve whispered in my ear.

"No—wait. Maybe." I stared hard at the big oak tree. "There!" I pointed. "I just saw a light on that side of the tree. Then it went out."

I dug my heels into the ground—planting them there firmly—so it would be harder to bolt, which is exactly what I wanted to do.

I cleared my throat.

"Who is there?" My voice squeaked.

The light flashed again.

Then it went out.

Crunch, crunch, crunch.

"D-did you hear that?" I asked Steve. He nodded.

Something was moving in the dark.

Crunch, crunch, crunch.

There it was again. Moving. Toward us.

I swung the flashlight around wildly. Trying to catch it in my beam.

Then I heard another sound. A voice. A laugh.

"Steve, did you hear that?" I whispered. "It laughed."

"Shine your light over there," Steve whispered back.

He sounded scared. I knew I was.

I swung my flashlight in its direction—and two human-like forms walked toward us.

Girls.

Two girls squinting in the light and giggling.

Two totally alive girls.

I wanted a ghost. Or a werewolf. Or a vampire. Even a mummy.

But no. I found girls.

"Who are you?" Steve asked as we walked toward them. "What are you doing out here?"

"I'm Kate Drennan," one of the girls answered in a soft voice. "And this is my sister, Betsy."

Both girls had bright blue eyes and long black hair. The one named Kate had straight hair tied back in a ponytail. The other one had wavy hair with curls that tumbled all the way down her back.

I'd never seen either of them before—even though they looked as though they should be in my grade.

"We were just—" Kate began again. But before she could finish, Betsy cut her off.

"Why do you get to ask the questions?" she demanded. "We have as much right to be here as you do."

"Okay, okay," I started to apologize. "It's just that I've never seen you around here before. Do you go to Shadyside Middle School?"

"No," Kate started to answer.

"We're on spring break," Betsy interrupted. "We go to school in Vermont. We don't know many kids in Shadyside, so it gets pretty boring."

"That's why we sneaked out tonight," Kate added. "We were bored. There was nothing on TV. Nothing to do."

"We sneaked out, too," I admitted.

Kate—the quieter one—smiled. And Betsy—the bossy one—seemed to relax a little.

"At least you get a vacation," Steve added. "We don't have one until school lets out for the summer."

"We should head back," Betsy said. "Our parents might check up on us or something."

"Us, too. We'll probably see you around," I volunteered. "We'll be out here a lot—we're going to rebuild that tree house."

I shone the flashlight up into the branches of the big dark oak. Both girls glanced up. Then I noticed Kate's expression. She looked scared. Really scared.

Betsy glared at me. "What did you say?" she asked.

"I said we're going to rebuild that old tree house."

"That's what I thought you said," Betsy replied. "But you can't."

"Why can't we?" Steve demanded.

"No one can," Betsy insisted.

Kate began chewing nervously on the end of her ponytail. "You can't rebuild the tree house," she said. "You can't because . . . because . . ."

"Because of the secret about it," Betsy finished for her sister.

"The secret?" I asked. "What secret?"

A tree house with a secret! Is this cool or what?

"We can't tell you. Everyone knows about this old tree house," Betsy snapped.

Then she narrowed her eyes. "But I *will* tell you this—if you don't want to get hurt . . . you'll stay away from the tree house!"

"They're just trying to scare us," Steve replied. "But it's not going to work. Right?"

"Right," I replied, not feeling as convinced as I sounded.

"Well, I—uh—really think you should listen to Betsy," Kate whispered. "Because we, um, we heard some kids tried to fix up the tree house and they . . ."

"What happened to them?" These girls were driving me crazy. "Did they die? What happened?"

Betsy shook her sister's shoulder, interrupting her for the millionth time. "Come on. Let's go. They don't need to hear that old story," she snapped. "If they're smart, they'll just stay away."

"Why? Why should we stay away?" I asked.

Then I remembered what I read about ghosts and cold spots. "Wow! I said. "Is the tree house haunted?"

"Come on, Kate," Betsy ordered. "These guys are hopeless."

Kate gave sort of a half smile. "We do have to go," she said. "Our mom will freak if she can't find us."

"Wait!" I protested. "Just tell us some more about the tree house. Please!"

I thought Kate was about to say something, but Betsy didn't give her a chance. "I said come *on*," she grumbled, tugging her sister across the clearing.

"Bye," Kate called over her shoulder.

As they stepped onto the path, Betsy stopped and called back, "Remember, you have been warned. Now if anything bad happens to you, it will be your own fault!"

The next day at school, I couldn't concentrate. Betsy's warning kept echoing in my head. What did it mean? What was the big secret about the tree house?

It must be haunted, I decided. That had to be it. At least I hoped so.

I spent the last part of the day—the part when we were supposed to be doing math—drawing tree house plans on the cover of my notebook.

In some of the plans, I sketched a shadowy figure sitting on the end of a branch. I made it shadowy because I didn't know what a ghost really looked like. Not yet, anyway.

As soon as the last bell rang, I raced home. I headed straight into the garage and loaded up two big cardboard boxes with nails, old boards, and lots of tools.

That was the easy part.

Next came the hard part—Steve. I found him lying on the couch, watching TV and munching Cheese Curlies.

"Come on," I said. "We have to start before it gets too dark out there."

Steve's eyes remained glued to the screen. "Let's wait till Saturday," he answered. "I want to watch the rest of this show."

I glanced at the TV. "You've seen that cartoon at least one hundred times!" I snatched the remote from his hand and clicked off the TV. "We had a deal."

"Our deal didn't say *when* I had to help," Steve answered. "What's the big rush, anyway?"

"I think the tree house is haunted! I think someone died up there! And I did see something in the shadows."

"Dylan," Steve said, shaking his head, "the only thing that died is your brain."

"I can *prove* to you that ghosts are real," I replied. "Just think about it—this is the perfect chance for us to settle our argument about ghosts. If the tree house is haunted, I know I can prove it."

Steve shoved himself up from the sofa.

"All right, Dylan, my lad. But if we don't see a ghost before we finish the tree house, you have to admit I was right and you were wrong."

"Sure. Let's go."

"And you have to stop talking about ghosts, reading about ghosts, watching movies about ghosts—even thinking about ghosts. Deal?" Steve asked.

"Deal," I agreed.

We headed to the garage to pick up the supplies. Steve chose the lightest box, of course.

We cut across the backyard, and I led the way into the woods. "Wow!" Steve cried as he stumbled along behind me. "The woods are even colder than last night. From now on, I'm wearing my winter parka when we come out here."

"It's because of the ghost," I informed him. "Haunted places usually have a colder temperature."

"Give me a break!" Steve shouted. "It's cold because of all the trees. The sunlight can't get through the branches."

After that we trudged along without talking. My box felt heavier with every step. I thought about turning around and asking Steve to trade. But I didn't want to start another argument.

I stopped when the path reached the clearing.

I scanned the shadows around the oak tree.

Nothing there.

I dumped my cardboard box on the ground. I turned to Steve—and couldn't believe what I saw. "Where's yours?" I demanded.

"Where's my what?" Steve asked, smiling.

"Your *box.*"

Steve took off his baseball cap, smoothed his hair, and stuck the cap back on. "I left it at the edge of the backyard. We couldn't possibly use all that junk in one day," Steve explained.

"That was not our deal!" I yelled. "Our deal was that you help. Watching me carry a box does not count as help. And neither does leaving our stuff behind!"

"Okay, okay. I'll get the box," Steve muttered.

I watched Steve disappear down the path—and realized what a big mistake I had made. I'd be lucky if Steve returned—with or without the box.

In fact, I knew exactly what Steve would do. He would decide he needed a glass of water. No, a glass of water and some more Cheese Curlies—to build up his strength. And since he couldn't eat and carry the box at the same time, he'd watch a few cartoons until he finished the Curlies. And by then, it would be time for me to go home.

Well, I didn't need Steve, anyway. I really didn't expect him to do much work. I just wanted him along because the woods were kind of creepy. Which is exactly what I started thinking as I opened the carton.

It was quiet here. Way too quiet.

And dark. Steve was right about the branches. They blocked out all the sunlight.

I glanced up at the tree house and felt a shiver race up and down my spine. You wanted to see a ghost, I told myself. And now's your chance.

I forced myself to march over to the tree. I tested the first rung of the ladder nailed onto the trunk. A little wobbly, but okay, I decided.

I stepped on the rung. It held me—no problem. I tugged on the second rung before I climbed up— it felt okay, too. Only three more rungs to go.

I stared up at the tree house again. An icy breeze swept over me and my knees began to shake.

Take a deep breath, I told myself. Don't wimp out now.

I stepped up to the next rung.

And that's when I heard the sound.

A sickening CRACK.

My feet flew out from under me as the third rung snapped off the trunk.

I flung my arms around the trunk. I kicked my legs wildly, searching for the next rung.

My heart pounded in my chest until my feet found it. Then I clung there for a few minutes. Hugging the tree trunk tightly, trying to catch my breath.

A cold gust of wind blew. My teeth began to chatter.

I inhaled deeply. "Okay, just one more rung to go," I said out loud. But I couldn't move. I remained frozen to the spot.

Then I pictured myself talking to Steve after I'd proven that ghosts exist. "Steve, my lad," I would say, "don't feel stupid. Even though you are a year older, no one expects you to be right about everything."

That gave me the courage to go on.

I made my way to the top rung. I peered underneath the tree house and studied the platform. Half of it was badly damaged. The boards were black and charred. But the other half appeared solid enough. I banged on it with my fist a few times just to make sure.

Then I pulled myself through the open trapdoor—and felt something touch my face. Something soft. Something airy. Something light.

I screamed.

I found the ghost!

About R. L. Stine

R. L. Stine, the creator of *Ghosts of Fear Street,* has written almost 100 scary novels for kids. The *Ghosts of Fear Street* series, like the *Fear Street* series, takes place in Shadyside and centers on the scary events that happen to people on Fear Street.

When he isn't writing, R. L. Stine likes to play pinball on his very own pinball machine, and explore New York City with his wife, Jane, and fifteen-year-old son, Matt.